Barney
The Boat Dog

Fairground Surprise

D0795176

To the two Johns, for their lovely covers and illustrations

First published in the UK in 2011 by Usborne Publishing Ltd., Usborne House,
83-85 Saffron Hill, London EC1N 8RT, England.
www.usborne.com

Cover illustration by John Butler, johnbutlerart.com
Illustrations by John Francis, courtesy of Bernard Thornton Artists, London

The name Usborne and the devices 🏮 🌐 are Trade Marks of
Usborne Publishing Ltd.

A CIP catalogue record for this book is available from the British Library.

ISBN 9781409522034

Fairground Surprise

Linda Newbery

Illustrated by John Francis

Chapter One

Barney loved it when Freddie came to stay on *Whistling Jack*. The rest of the time, it was just Barney and Jim and their narrowboat, and Barney loved that too. The waterways took them through peaceful countryside, to riverside towns, and sometimes even through a busy city, with locks so narrow that the boat could only just squeeze through. On their journeys they met all sorts of people: old friends, new friends, and strangers. Barney never knew where they'd go next, or who they might meet.

But the times when Freddie was with them were always special. Freddie was Jim's little grandson. Sometimes his parents came to visit, too; but the boat wasn't big enough for everyone to sleep on it, so more often it was just Freddie who stayed for a few days. Freddie was good fun. He played running and chasing games with Barney; in hot weather he'd paddle in the shallows and look for fish, and encourage Barney to swim.

Freddie was used to the waterways now, and liked being crew for Jim. Whenever they reached a lock, Freddie was nearly as clever as Barney at knowing what to do. As soon as the boat pulled over to the bank, Barney would jump ashore and Freddie would scramble, and they'd head for the lock with the special handle that opened and closed the sluice gates. Sometimes, with Jim close by, Freddie was allowed to take a turn at steering the boat. Barney stood by Freddie's legs, making sure he did everything right.

This Easter holiday, Jim was taking
Freddie and Barney to the spring fair at
Ripplestead. Just now they were on a
stretch of water that passed through

meadows, where sheep and cows grazed.
Jim was at the back of the boat, steering,
while Freddie and Barney looked out from
the front deck.

Freddie had a secret to share with Barney. He fetched something he'd hidden underneath the bunk beds, and brought it out to the deck. Before showing Barney, he glanced round to make quite sure Jim couldn't see from where he was standing. But the whole length of the roof was between them, and Jim was concentrating hard on guiding the boat. Willow branches grew low over the canal just here, and Jim had to steer carefully past them.

"Look!" Freddie held up a pink plastic pig, fat and round, with a tail that twizzled into a tight curl.

Barney gave a little *whuff*, and Freddie shushed him.

"My piggy bank! I've been saving up for a birthday present for Grandad. He mustn't see. But I need to count my money – I'm going to buy something at the fair."

As he turned the pig upside down, there was a heavy slide and clink of coins inside it. Freddie held it higher and tried to peer through the slot on its back. Just then, dangling willow twigs brushed the roof of *Whistling Jack*, and the pig was swept right out of Freddie's grasp. He lunged, grabbed, and for a moment the pig seemed to balance on his outstretched hands…but then it toppled and fell into the shallows with a heavy *plosh*.

"*Oh no!*" Freddie exclaimed. "My pig! All my money!"

With his front paws on the side of the boat, Barney barked sharply, his eyes on the pig, and the place where it had fallen.

The edge of the canal was muddy here, and a group of young cows had come down to the water's edge to drink. Their hooves churned up a muddy swirl. Two of them snorted and dashed back as the pink pig floated towards them. Although it was heavy with coins, the rounded pink top of it was clear of the shallow water. Barney was about to jump overboard to the rescue when Freddie grabbed his collar.

"No, Barney, don't! Jim mustn't see."

Jim *hadn't* seen; Barney looked, and Jim was busy edging *Whistling Jack* past another narrowboat, *Dabchick*, that was coming the other way.

"Bit of a wait at the lock there," the man steering *Dabchick* called to Jim.

"Okay. Thanks," Jim answered. Then he called along the deck to Freddie, "We're nearly at Mudpool Wharf. We'll moor up here – I need to top up the water."

"Okay!" Freddie shouted, then

whispered to Barney, "See? I'll run back
and fetch it, no trouble."

Barney dashed through to the rear
deck in order to keep sight of the pig,
which bobbed slightly in the shallows.

Some way behind *Whistling Jack*, another
narrowboat was coming along. A girl stood
on the front deck, and as her boat
approached the cattle-drinking place

Barney saw her point at something, then turn round to shout. The boat slowed and pulled over, frightening the cows, who turned and ran up the bank, snorting and scrabbling, kicking up mud.

The man at the tiller reached for a boathook that lay along the roof, but the girl was quicker; she jumped down, her spotted wellies splashing into the water. She reached for the pig, and held it up, dripping.

Then she pulled herself back on board, shouted to the man who was steering, and the boat moved on.

Barney gave two sharp barks, to alert Freddie. But Freddie was inside the boat now, making his way through to the rear deck – he hadn't seen.

At Mudpool Wharf, narrowboats were moored on both sides, and two were waiting to go through the lock gates.

Jim looked at his watch. "Time for

elevenses, after I've filled up."

When the mooring-ropes were tied, and Jim was busy uncoiling the hose and filling *Whistling Jack's* water tank, Freddie told him, "Won't be a minute!" and set off back the way they'd come. Barney galloped beside him, ears flapping. He knew that Freddie was going back to look for the pig; and he also knew that Freddie wouldn't find it. As they ran past the boat with the girl on it, which was still chugging down the canal, a woman reading on the front deck waved and shouted a friendly "Hello there!", the way boat-people often call out to people on the towpath. The girl in spotted wellies, now sitting on the roof, waved too, but Freddie was running too hard to notice.

Barney stopped dead – he'd seen Freddie's pig! It was upturned next to the girl, propped between plant-pots, all four pink feet in the air. Barney gave a yip, but Freddie was in too much of a hurry to stop.

The pig glided past, towards *Whistling Jack*.

"Here's the place," Freddie puffed, as they reached the muddy slope where the cows had stood. The ground was all churned and hoof-marked; the water nudged gently at the shore in little ripples. Freddie looked and looked; he found a stick and poked among the reeds, but he didn't find the pig. Of course he didn't. Barney turned to face the other boat, which was now drawing close to *Whistling Jack*; he wanted Freddie to look that way too.

But Freddie only looked gloomy, and started to trudge back towards the boat. "*Now* what, Barney? Grandad gave me that piggy bank for Christmas, and I've gone and lost it. And all my money! I've been saving my pocket money for *ages* – I wanted to get Grandad a present at the fair!"

Barney rushed forward and woofed – doing all he could to show Freddie where the pig was. He pointed his ears and his nose towards the other boat; he made little dashes; he looked round at Freddie, wanting him to follow.

Freddie jabbed his stick into the mud. "It's not funny, Barney," he said, downcast. "What will I do now?"

Chapter Two

As Jim finished coiling up the hose,
Pernickety went past. On the front deck
a woman sat reading a book; she didn't
notice Jim, but the man at the tiller
waved to him, and so did a girl in
daisy-spotted wellies, who was sitting
on the roof.

Jim looked round for Freddie and Barney. There they were, on the towpath: Freddie walking glumly, Barney trotting ahead.

"What's up?" Jim called.

"Oh – nothing!" Freddie answered.

"Barney wanted a little run, that's all."

"I've put the kettle on," said Jim. "I'm

making you hot chocolate, and I've got a nice packet of biscuits. We'll have a little break before we go through the lock."

"Okay," said Freddie. "I'll just go and look at the boats first."

Pernickety had moved up towards the lock gates. It was a very short and narrow lock, with room for only one narrowboat at a time, and *Pernickety* had to wait until another boat, *Ruby Tuesday*, came through from the other direction.

When *Pernickety* entered the lock, Freddie moved alongside to watch. *Pernickety* sank lower and lower as the water gushed through the lower sluices. There was a man at the tiller; a woman and a girl were working the gates. Freddie

wondered why Barney kept nudging his
legs – but then he saw his pig.

His pig!

His mouth opened in astonishment.
There it was, on the roof of *Pernickety*,
wedged upside down with its pink feet in
the air! He almost yelled out, "Hey! That's
mine!" but stopped, because the man at
the tiller looked a bit cross. He reminded

Freddie of the rather strict Year 6 teacher at his school, Mr. Fisher. This man *wasn't* Mr. Fisher, but he did look as if he could get very cross indeed. He was huffing to himself, and shouting "Hurry up!" to the woman and the girl, as if they could make the water flow faster. "There's another boat waiting."

"What shall I do, Barney?" Freddie whispered.

He couldn't just sit and watch while his pig was kidnapped. Pignapped! But perhaps they'd only meant to rescue it, and would give it back if he asked.

"Excuse me!" he shouted to the man.

But there was too much engine noise for anyone to hear him, and the man was facing the other way. The pig was so close, almost within reach now, as the water level dropped, that Freddie had a better idea. He needn't bother anyone – just grab the pig and quickly get it back on board *Whistling Jack*. Grandad would be busy with mugs and biscuits and kettle, and needn't know what had happened.

The *Pernickety* girl and woman were standing by the lock gates; the man was at the tiller. Could he grab the piggy bank without being seen?

The girl and her mother started to push at the heavy lever that opened the lower gate. To do this, they'd turned their backs on the boat; and the man steering was leaning out to the far side, watching them.

Now!

"Barney, you wait here," said Freddie

into Barney's ear; then he took his chance.
He dropped lightly onto the roof, landing
among the flowerpots.

He picked up the pig, then turned to jump
back ashore.

Too late! The water level had dropped
faster than he'd expected. Already,

Pernickety was much lower; the lock-side
was high above, and the iron ladder too far
away to reach. Barney's worried face was
peering over the edge. Freddie clutched
the pig, certain that at any moment the
man would see, and shout at him.

What now?

If he just waited, the boat would have
to stop again, to let its crew climb aboard.
Maybe he'd edge along the roof and ask
the man to let him get off; or, better still,
he'd slip ashore unnoticed. Meanwhile,
he hid himself and the pig behind a
tarpaulin that was rolled up on the roof.
He'd be back on *Whistling Jack* before
Grandad even noticed he was gone.

But it all happened so quickly! The
man steered towards the bank, the girl

and her mum stepped on, and the boat was pulling away again.

Freddie huddled by the tarpaulin, feeling very silly. Why had he done such a stupid thing?

The girl and the woman had gone right through the boat to the front deck. If they turned round, they'd see him.

"Not far now," shouted the man. "Ripplestead in half an hour, I'd say."

"Good!" said the girl to her mother. "We'll soon be at the fair."

So they were going there too! Freddie's thoughts raced. If only Grandad would come along behind, everything would be all right. But of course Grandad would start looking for him, and would be worried, and wouldn't leave his mooring.

How could he let Grandad know what had happened?

Freddie looked at the smiley face of the pig, as if it might have a suggestion to make. He was a stowaway now, though he hadn't intended to be.

The mother had moved to the hatchway.

"I'm going inside to wash up. Come and help?"

"Okay," said the girl, but just then the father called out from the back.

"Jenna! There's that dog again, the one we saw at the lock!"

Freddie risked a peep. There on the towpath was Barney, trotting fast to keep up with the boat. Freddie was relieved he was here, but how could Barney help?

Freddie curled himself up again, his heart beating fast. Should he crawl out and reveal himself as a stowaway? He felt a bit sneaky now, for hiding. Why hadn't he simply asked for his pig back? If only he had, he'd be with Grandad and Barney now, on *Whistling Jack*, and everything would be fine.

How had he got himself into such a muddle?

Chapter Three

"Freddie?" Jim called. "Freddie?"

Freddie's mug of steaming hot chocolate was waiting, and Jim had made coffee for himself, and he'd opened the packet of biscuits: chocolate chip, Freddie's favourite. But where *was* Freddie?

He looked towards the lock. *Pernickety*

must have gone down through the lock, because another boat was now waiting to go through, but Jim couldn't see Freddie. Had Freddie and Barney come back on board while he was busy in the kitchen?

Jim stooped to call through the open door. Maybe Freddie had gone into the cabin for something? But there was no answer.

Panic clutched at Jim's chest. Could Freddie be hiding, for a joke? Freddie did like games. But what if he'd fallen in the water, and no one had seen? Freddie was a good little swimmer and the water wasn't very deep, but still it was cold and murky, swirled about by the boats' propellers—

No! Jim couldn't bear to think about it. And with all those boats about, Freddie couldn't have fallen in unnoticed. There must be some simple explanation.

Bewildered, he climbed ashore, and looked into the water and along the towpath in both directions. "Freddie?" he shouted. "Freddie?"

Then something else struck him. "Barney? Barney? Where are you?"

A man in walking boots was sitting on a stile by the towpath, drinking coffee from a flask. "Lost someone?"

"Yes," said Jim. "A little boy – my grandson. Dark hair, jeans, red sweatshirt. Have you seen him?"

The man nodded. "Saw him getting on another boat. The one that went through the lock five or ten minutes ago."

"Really?" Jim was so astonished that he

wondered if the man could be telling the truth. Why would Freddie do such a thing? He was usually such a sensible boy.

"Course, I didn't think anything of it," said the man. "Thought he *belonged* to that boat. *Pernickety* was its name. I noticed that."

Jim needed to hurry; *Pernickety* would be some way ahead by now. He thanked the man, then said, "Come on, Bar—" before remembering that Barney was missing, too. "You didn't see my dog, did you? Little terrier, white with brown patches?"

The man pointed along the towpath. "Went running after the boat, he did."

Jim thanked him, climbed back on board *Whistling Jack*, and started the engine. What was going on? He didn't understand at all.

Barney, too, was puzzled by Freddie's behaviour. All he knew was that he'd better keep an eye on things. He trotted along briskly, keeping pace with *Pernickety*.

Where *was* Freddie? Barney had seen him jump down to the roof, but now he'd vanished. He could see the man steering, and the girl and the mum were inside by one of the windows, but he couldn't see Freddie, outside or in. He must be hiding, as he often did on *Whistling Jack*, for a game. But there was something odd about this.

He heard the dad say, "The dog's still here! He thinks he's coming with us!"

The mum came out to the rear deck to see for herself. "He looks like a clever little dog! Wasn't he with that boy we saw, running along the towpath? I think they're from the boat we passed at the lock."

"*Whistling Jack*, it was called," said the dad. "I know that name from somewhere, I'm sure I do!"

Barney didn't understand *every*thing people said, but he picked up quite a lot. And he certainly knew the name *Whistling Jack*. When he heard the man say it, he ran to face him, and gave a little *gruff*.

The mum laughed. "See, I told you he was clever! He heard you say the name of his boat. But what does he want?"

"Hey! Dog!" called the girl, standing on the steps. "Are you lost?"

Barney gave a sharp plaintive bark.

Freddie? Freddie! he tried to signal. *Where's Freddie?*

From his hiding place, Freddie heard the mum's voice again. "Jenna! We forgot all about the piggy bank! We were going to hand it in at the lock-keeper's cottage, weren't we?"

The girl clapped a hand to her mouth,

then clambered up to the roof, her feet clomping close to Freddie.

"But where *is* it?" she called to her mum. "Have you moved it?"

"No! Haven't touched it."

"It can't have fallen in! I wedged it carefully," said Jenna, on all fours.

"Are you sure you didn't take it inside?"

"I didn't!" Jenna answered. "At least, I don't *think* I did. We'd better look, just in case."

Freddie heard them moving along inside the boat, and the dad saying, "What, the pig's disappeared?"

"It *must* be on the roof!" said Jenna, emerging onto the rear deck. "I'll have another look."

Freddie hunched himself as small as he

could. Jenna's spotted wellies came close and closer until they were centimetres from his nose; then, suddenly, she crouched down. Freddie found himself looking at a pair of bright brown eyes that stared straight back, round with astonishment.

For a moment, neither he nor Jenna spoke. Then she whispered: "Who are you? What are you *doing*?"

"I'm Freddie. Just collecting my pig, that's all."

To his surprise, a big grin spread across Jenna's face. "Oooh, you're a stowaway! A pig-rescuer and secret stowaway! I *love* secrets. Don't move, Freddie. Don't say a word. I'll make sure you stay hidden."

"But I—"

Jenna put a finger to her lips. "It's my

dad, you see. He's very fierce. He eats stowaways for breakfast, or if he's in a good mood he just throws them overboard. Don't worry. You'll be fine, as long as you do what I say."

She was playing a game with him – Freddie hoped so, anyway. He might have enjoyed playing along, if it hadn't been for Grandad, with *Whistling Jack* way behind now, on the other side of the lock.

"Can't I get off?"

"We'll be stopping again soon. Where are you going, then?" Jenna asked.

"Back the other way. To *Whistling Jack*."

"The boat we saw near the lock?"

"Yes. My grandad's there. It's his boat. And Barney—" Freddie looked towards the bank, where Barney was still trotting along, looking a little tired now. "Barney's my grandad's dog. He's here because I'm here. We're going to the fair at Ripplestead, only Grandad's back there and he doesn't know where I am."

"That's all right!" said Jenna, who had the look of someone not easily worried. "We'll phone him and say you'll meet him at the fair. We're heading there too. Has he got a mobile?" She reached into her dungarees pocket and took out hers. "D'you know his number?"

"I can just about remember it," said Freddie, thinking hard. "Mum made me learn it."

"You'll have to make sure no one hears." Jenna handed him her mobile, and tugged the tarpaulin a little further over his head.

She was weird, this girl, but at least he was
going to talk to Grandad! He entered the
number, hoping he'd got it right; the
ringtone had hardly sounded before
Grandad answered, sounding frantic.

"Grandad, it's me," Freddie whispered.

Chapter Four

Jim felt giddy with relief; so giddy that he wasn't quite sure he'd got everything quite clear. But Freddie was safe! That was the main thing. He held on to that.

"On another boat? But *why*?"

"Tell you later." Freddie sounded as if he was whispering. "I'll see you at the fair. This boat's going there too. *Pernickety*, it's called."

"Who are you with? Are they – can't I – is Barney—"

"I've got to finish now, Grandad. Yes, Barney's here too. See you in a bit."

"Wait for me on the towpath when you get there," Jim said quickly; but the phone had gone silent. He looked at it, held it to his ear, gazed at it again. He found the number and pressed the green telephone key to call back, but no one answered – the phone, whoever's it was, must have been turned off. Freddie hadn't got a mobile phone of his own.

Jim was baffled, but there was no point sitting here puzzling – he needed to get himself and *Whistling Jack* along to the fair as soon as he could. He steered out to the middle of the canal, and opened the throttle. A group of ducks that had been dabbling nearby took fright, and lifted off into the air with loud *waaaaks* and whirring of wings.

Barney was in a bit of a dither. He was tired, too, having trotted along the bank for some way at a fast pace. He wasn't at all sure he was doing the right thing. He knew for sure that Freddie was on board the other boat; he'd heard him talking to the girl, in a hushed voice. What was going on, and why, he had no idea.

What Barney did know was that *Whistling Jack* was nowhere in sight, and that he'd run off and left Jim, which was

Bad. But he'd done it in order to keep sight of Freddie, which was Good. Good and Bad jostled for position in his head; he couldn't tell which was winning. Was he being a good dog or a bad dog, and could he be both at once? He usually tried to be good, and on the rare occasions he was bad, he didn't much enjoy it.

Should he stay as near as he could to Freddie, or go back and find Jim? He

couldn't do *both*. Barney gave a little whine, and sat down to think about it. *Pernickety* chugged on round the next bend, out of sight.

* * *

"…So you see," Freddie was telling Jenna, still on the roof of *Pernickety*, "that's why I didn't want Grandad to know. It's tomorrow, his birthday, and I wanted to give him a surprise present."

"From the fair!" said Jenna. "I need to get something, too. We'll go together and see what we can find."

"All right up there, Jenna?" called the dad. "You're very quiet!"

"Yes!" shouted Jenna. "It's okay, I've found the pig!"

Freddie glared at her. "What did you say that for? It's *my* pig!"

"Good!" the dad called back. "There's another lock-keeper's cottage past Ripplestead. We'll hand it in there."

"No problem," Jenna said quietly to Freddie. "We won't. You'll be back with your grandad by then, with his special present. How much money's in that pig?"

"I'm not—" Freddie started to say, but then noticed something, and craned his neck to look. "Barney! Barney's not with us any more! Poor old Barney, he must have got tired, keeping up."

"He'll be okay," Jenna told him. "He'll sit down and wait for your grandad, I expect. Now – the money?"

Freddie held the pig upside down and tried to peer through the slot.

"There's an easier way, silly." Jenna took the pig from him, and showed him a plastic plug under its tummy that could be taken out. When she did that, coins gushed out in a tinkling slither. "Looks like quite a lot!"

Together they arranged
the coins in piles,
and counted them
up. But a lot of
the coins were
pennies and two
pences and fives, and

Freddie was disappointed. "It doesn't add
up to as much as I thought! I hope there's
enough to buy Grandad something nice."

"You can win things, too, at the fair," said
Jenna. "I'll help. I'm good at winning things."

"Thanks," said Freddie, wondering if
there might be a chance to win something
himself. He tipped the money into the
zipped pocket of his sweatshirt.

"We're here!" shouted Jenna's dad, from

the rear deck. As they rounded a bend, Ripplestead Wharf came into view, busy with boats and people. In a field a short distance from the canal, Freddie saw striped marquees, colourful pagodas and stalls. Jolly music wafted across. There was a bouncy castle and a helter-skelter, and a whirling ride with swing-seats that flew high into the air, with people whooping and screaming as they clung to their seats and each other.

Freddie had never seen such an old-fashioned funfair, but Grandad had told him all about it – the roundabout horses and the coconut shy, the puppet show and the candyfloss.

Jenna's dad cruised slowly past the moored boats, looking for a place to tie up.

"It's so busy!" called Jenna's mum. "I think we'll have to go on past, and walk back."

"I've got an idea!" Jenna whispered to Freddie, as they waited on the front deck. She scrambled up to the roof, and shouted to her parents, "Oh, but I can't *wait*! Couldn't you pull over by those steps, and drop me off? I'll only look round, promise, and I won't get into trouble."

"Best if we all go together," her dad

called back, but the mum said, "It won't do any harm, will it? Jenna, you've got your mobile, haven't you? Make sure it's turned on, and meet us by the helter-skelter in fifteen minutes."

"See? Mum always lets me do what I want," Jenna told Freddie. She took her mobile phone out of her pocket, and thumbed the *on* key. "Now, I'll make a bit of a fuss, and as soon as he pulls in, you jump ashore. Wait for me by that gate. Okay?"

Freddie watched carefully as the boat nosed in alongside a *PRIVATE – NO MOORING* sign. Jenna went through to the rear deck, ready to step off; then she felt in both pockets, and exclaimed, "Oh, no! Where's my purse? I had it earlier. I can't go to the fair without it!"

While her mum and dad were busy suggesting where it might be, and helping her to look, Freddie climbed ashore and ran towards the gate that led into the fair. When he looked back, moments later, he saw Jenna jogging up behind, and *Pernickety* pulling away to find a mooring place.

"See? Easy," said Jenna, triumphant.

Only then did Freddie think of something. The money was safely in his pocket now, but the pig was still on the roof of *Pernickety*, where he'd left it.

Chapter Five

Barney was worried now. He'd stopped
to get his breath back, and *Pernickety*
had gone on out of sight. All he'd done
was make things worse. He wasn't keeping
an eye on Freddie any more. He wasn't
with Jim, either. So that made *two* things
that were Bad, without a single Good to

set against them.

What should he do?

He'd better hurry back and find Jim as soon as he could. He stood up, and forced his tired legs to carry on running. Soon he gave a happy *whuff* as he saw *Whistling Jack* coming round the next bend, with Jim watching anxiously from the rear deck.

"*Barney!*" Jim shouted, and pulled over to the bank. Barney hurled himself over the side into Jim's arms, where he licked and wriggled and wagged. *Something* was right, at least.

Freddie looked at his watch. It would take *Whistling Jack* a little while to catch up, he guessed, and in that time he could buy Grandad's birthday present and be back at the towpath to meet him. Yes, that would work, as long as he found the right present quickly enough. Then he and Grandad could go back to the fair together for as long as they wanted. As for the pig... perhaps Jenna would fetch it for him later.

"Great!" said Jenna. "Now we've got some time to ourselves. Let's go and look for the things we need."

"What do *you* need?"

"Oh, something for Mum and Dad," said Jenna, walking briskly. "There are lots of stalls here – we'll see what we can find. We can go on the rides later."

As well as the helter-skelter, the roundabout, dodgem cars and the whirly ride, there were lots of stalls, selling children's toys, sweets, china animals,

jewellery, and things to eat. The air was
full of the sugar-sweetness of candyfloss
and the oniony waft of hot dogs.

Freddie gazed at one stall after another.
What should he choose for Grandad? Only
now did he realize that he had no idea.

Then he saw a stall that sold hats.

"There!" He pointed to a peaked tweed

cap at the back of the stall. Grandad would like that. He sometimes wore a cap, when the weather was bad. This could be a smart cap for winter.

"That one? How much is it?" Jenna asked the stallholder, who looked at the label and said, "Ten pounds."

Ten pounds! That was far more than Freddie's piggy bank savings. He turned away, disappointed.

"I'll just have to get him some sweets. He likes mint humbugs."

"I can't see what I want, either," said Jenna. "Let's try the hoopla."

"What's hoopla?"

"Haven't you ever seen it?" Jenna said. "You throw hoops to win things. I expect they'll have good prizes there."

* * *

Jim felt a bit better now that he had Barney with him again, standing next to him as he steered. But it also gave him a new worry, knowing that Barney wasn't with Freddie any more. Had something happened?

"What's going on, Barney boy? Where's our Freddie?" Jim asked Barney, who gave a little whine and a wiggle.

"If only you could talk!" Jim thought, as he often did. Sometimes there was no mistaking what Barney meant, but at other times Jim could only try to guess.

There were so many boats at Ripplestead, taking up all the mooring places! There was nowhere to stop. Jim had to take *Whistling Jack* some way past, looking for a place, looking for *Pernickety*, and for Freddie waiting on the bank.

At last, his heart leaped as he saw *Pernickety*, and a space to moor up just in front of it. But there was no sign of Freddie, nor of anyone else. Jim began to worry all over again as he tied *Whistling Jack*'s mooring-ropes. Where was Freddie now? He climbed ashore, looking closely at the other boat. It was locked up; no one here at all.

Barney had seen something. He stood alertly on the bank, nose and ears pointing at the roof. Jim looked, and saw a pink piggy bank lying on its side by a rolled tarpaulin.

"What, Barney boy? That pig? That's just like the piggy bank I gave Freddie at Christmas! Is it the same one? But what's it doing *here*, with no sign of Freddie?"

He didn't like this at all! He looked in all directions; he stared into the canal, fearful all over again that Freddie might have fallen in. He kept reminding himself that Freddie was a sensible boy, and wouldn't do anything silly. At least, Jim didn't *think* he would.

Barney was eager to go to the fair. He made little dashes in that direction, turning round to see if Jim was following.

Yes, thought Jim, the most likely explanation was that Freddie had gone on ahead. It would be hard to resist a funfair! And Barney seemed to know something.

"All right, Barney boy," said Jim. "We'll

go and look."

The fairground was busy now. As they walked past the stalls and rides, Jim kept scanning the crowd for Freddie's red sweatshirt. At least he'd stand out, wearing such a bright colour.

Barney whuffed, and led Jim purposefully towards the helter-skelter. Several children were sliding and skidding down the spiral slide, mouths wide open in joyful fright. But Freddie wasn't one of them.

A man and a woman stood waiting. Barney seemed to recognize them, and was trying to make Jim hurry. Approaching, Jim saw that the man wore a navy-blue cap with *Pernickety* in stitched letters above the peak.

"Clever boy, Barney," Jim puffed, and as soon as they were close enough he called,

"Er, excuse me, is Freddie with you?"

The man and woman both looked blank. "Freddie?"

"My grandson," said Jim. "Quite small. Bright red sweatshirt. Mischievous face. Dark hair. Wasn't he on your boat?"

The woman shook her head. "No! Don't know who you mean. We haven't got a boy on our boat, just Jenna."

"We're waiting for our daughter," the man explained.

"But I had a phone call!" said Jim. "He said he was with you. On *Pernickety*."

"No," said the man, and "Definitely not," added the woman, both looking puzzled now – almost as puzzled as Jim felt.

"There can't be two boats called *Pernickety*!" said the woman, bending down to pat Barney. "But we did see your little dog, earlier. He was trotting along the towpath as if he wanted to be with us."

"You're with *Whistling Jack*, aren't you?" the man asked Jim. "We saw you back at the lock."

"That's right," said Jim miserably.

"I'm Dan, and this is Polly. Pleased to meet you."

"Oh. You too. I'm Jim," said Jim, so worried that it was an effort even to be polite.

He looked down at the ground, his eyes blurring with panic. He knew he must make himself calm. There must be some explanation!

"Oh dear, oh dear," he muttered. "Wherever can he be?"

Chapter Six

At the hoopla stall, Jenna clutched
Freddie's arm. "Ooo, I can see just what I
want. Oh, I've got to win it! Can you see
something for your grandad?"

Freddie looked at the prizes lined up on
a shelf at the back of the small tent. There
was a big doll in a patchwork dress, a jar of

toffees, some painted canalware; there was a teddy bear in a bow tie, a jigsaw puzzle with a picture of narrowboats, a huge chocolate Easter egg in a box, and lots of smaller things.

"The jigsaw puzzle! Grandad likes jigsaws. We do them on the boat, on dark nights in winter. That looks like a good one."

"Go on, then," Jenna told him. "You go first."

"Fancy a try?" said the man at the stall. "Fifty pence for six throws. Score with one,

69

you get a small prize. Score with three, choose whatever you want."

Freddie wasn't sure. What if he spent fifty pence and won nothing? Then there'd be even less of his money for Grandad's present.

"Come on, Freddie," Jenna urged. "You can't lose."

Freddie thought he could *easily* lose, but he very badly wanted to win a prize, especially with Jenna watching. He took a fifty-pence piece out of his pocket and handed it to the man, who gave him six rubber rings in return.

"Good lad. Stand on this chalk line here, see, and off you go."

There were twelve short poles stuck in the ground. Freddie angled himself, scowled, and threw his first ring. It missed, and flopped to the grass. The second one missed too. The third looped itself round a pole; Jenna cheered and clapped. The fourth hit a pole but bounced away, and the next two missed altogether.

"Well done, laddie. Here's your prize." The man handed him a ballpoint pen.

"But I wanted the jigsaw!"

The man grinned. "You need three for that. Why not have another go, now you've got your eye in?"

"Wait," said Jenna. "I'll get it for you. We'll pay half each. Have you got twenty-five pence?"

Freddie found two ten-pence pieces and a five, and handed them over rather doubtfully. At this rate, all his money would be gone, and he'd have nothing for Grandad apart from a cheap pen. That wasn't much of a present!

Jenna stood on the line, taking a moment to angle herself, plant her feet firmly, and stare at the poles. The first ring floated from her hand and landed neatly over the nearest one. Her second ring did the same. And the third.

"Three scores for a prize, right?" she said to the man, with the remaining three rings still in her hand.

"Okay. Well done. What will you have?"

"I'll have the jigsaw, thanks."

The man lifted the box down from the shelf and gave it to Jenna, who passed it straight to Freddie.

"Wow, thanks!" He clasped it to his chest.

Jenna squared up again. "Now, let's see what I can do with the other three."

Freddie looked at the other prizes lined up on the shelf. Which one did Jenna want? She didn't seem like the sort of girl who liked dolls, or even teddy bears.

It seemed that Jenna couldn't miss! One, two, three – the rings flew from her hand, each falling neatly over the furthest of the poles. A small crowd had gathered, and there was a round of applause when she'd finished. Jenna bowed modestly.

"Well done. You're too flipping good, you are," said the man. "Okay, what d'you want this time?"

"I'll take the teapot, please," said Jenna.

"The teapot? Sure?"

"Yes, the teapot. Thanks very much."

"What d'you want a boring old teapot for?" Freddie asked, as they walked away with their prizes. "I'd have had the Easter egg if I were you."

"It's not just any old teapot!" Jenna held it out proudly. It was a canalware

one – big, bright green, painted with large flowers in red and white. "See, what happened, I broke Mum's special teapot the other day, so I wanted to get her something to make up for it. Never thought I'd find an actual teapot as good as this!"

"It'll hold an awful lot of tea," said Freddie.

"Oh, but that's not the point!"

Freddie had no idea what she meant by that; but before he had time to ask, the phone in Jenna's pocket trilled out a happy little tune.

Chapter Seven

"Come on, Barney," said Jim, by the helter-skelter. "There's no point waiting here. I'm going to look for Freddie on the towpath," he told the *Pernickety* people. "I thought he'd be waiting for me there."

"I do hope you find him," Polly said anxiously.

About to set off, Jim thought he'd try phoning again, though without much hope.

This time, a girl's voice answered. "Hello?"

"Who's that?" Jim said quickly. "Is Freddie there?"

"Yes! Here he is," said the voice; and at the same moment, Barney pricked his ears, gave a sharp *whuff*, and shot off across the field at top speed.

"Hello, Grandad!" said Freddie, on the phone.

Jim was so relieved that his legs nearly gave way underneath him. As his eyes followed Barney, he saw Freddie coming towards him, phone to his ear, walking next to a girl in dungarees and wellies.

"I'm really sorry, Grandad," said

Freddie's voice in Jim's ear. But now Jim was hurrying to meet him, and there was no need for the phone, and Barney was running round behind Freddie's and Jenna's ankles, herding them as if they were a flock of sheep.

"Oh, here's Jenna at last!" said Polly. "And is that your Freddie?"

They all came together in the middle of the field, in a welter of questions and exclamations and hugs, and leapings and lickings from Barney. Freddie tried to hide the jigsaw puzzle behind his back, but then dropped it, and had to hastily snatch it up again.

Grandad didn't seem to notice; he gave Freddie a big cuddle. "Where've you *been* all this time?"

Freddie felt his face go hot. "Er…on *Pernickety*, like I said."

"You were on our boat?" exclaimed Jenna's dad.

"He was a secret stowaway," said Jenna.

Her dad looked very stern. "I think you two have got a bit of explaining to do."

But Grandad was far too relieved to be cross. When he and Jenna's parents had heard the whole story, he said: "But why didn't you just *say*? We'd have asked for the pig back and saved all this trouble!"

"Well, umm, you see," Freddie told him, "one thing sort of led to another. I didn't mean any of it to happen, not really."

"Jenna!" said her dad, who did after all seem very much like strict Mr. Fisher at school. "What were you thinking? You should have had more sense! Look at all the trouble you've made."

For a few seconds Freddie thought they were both going to get a real telling-off. Jenna looked downcast, but only for a moment. Then she handed the teapot to her mother, who took it in both hands, and laughed.

"Jenna! How clever of you to find that – it's just perfect! We'll certainly make good use of it."

"Grandad, this is for you." Freddie held out the jigsaw puzzle; it was impossible to hide it, and it was only a day early for his birthday. Grandad was delighted. He thanked and hugged Freddie, and showed the narrowboat picture to Jenna's mum and dad, and said that it would keep him and Freddie out of mischief.

Everything was going to be all right. Freddie bent down to pick up Barney. They were all together again, and the grown-ups seemed to be making friends.

"I've been trying to remember where I've heard the name *Whistling Jack* before," Jenna's dad was saying to Grandad, "and now I think I've got it. You used to live next door to my aunt and uncle, didn't you? With the canal running past the end of the garden?"

Jim stared at him. "What – you're Bill and Betty's nephew? Dan! Of course! I remember you when you were a little boy. You fell in the canal, once, and I helped fish you out."

"Did you, Dad?" said Jenna in delight.

"More than once, actually," said Dan; then he told Jim, "it's thanks to you we've come on this narrowboat holiday! I used to see *Whistling Jack* moored at the end of your garden, and thought how nice it would be to set off in a boat. So we've hired one for the week, and here we are."

"Jim," said Polly, "when we've all finished at the funfair, why don't you and Freddie come and have tea with us on *Pernickety*? Barney too, of course. It can be a sort of early birthday party."

Chapter Eight

After all his worry, Jim had a lovely
afternoon, and so did everyone else. Jenna
and Freddie went on all the rides, and
Jenna's mum rode a roundabout horse;
Barney found another dog to play chase-
and-yap with, Jim and Dan chatted away
about old times, and they all had ice cream.

Then Jim had a go at the tombola and won a big bottle of ginger beer, so he had something to add to the birthday tea on *Pernickety* when they all went back there.

They squashed in round the little table. Dan made tea, and poured ginger beer for Freddie and Jenna, and Polly cut up a cherry cake.

Jim was puzzled, looking at the blue-and-white striped teapot on the table. "I thought you'd be using the new teapot?"

"No!" Jenna sounded quite shocked. "It's not for tea."

"It's much more important than that,"
Dan said. He reached up into the little
cupboard above the window, and brought
down a small box. He opened it to show
Jim and Freddie what was inside –
coloured counters in red, yellow, blue and
green. "This is what we use our special
teapot for."

"Tiddlywinks?" said Jim.

"Tiddlywinks!" agreed Dan. "Our
favourite game."

"We always flip them into a teapot," said
Polly. "But there was, er, a little accident
the other night—"

"*My* little accident," said Jenna. "And
Mum's favourite tiddlywinking teapot got
smashed into bits. But now we've got this
one. It's lovely, and it's canalware, so it

won't ever break. Perfect!"

"So," said Dan, "what are we waiting for? Will you play, Jim? Freddie?"

Barney had never seen a game of tiddlywinks, but he thought it was greatly exciting. When Dan had explained the rules about squidgers, winks and tiddlies, the first round began.

There wasn't much space, with the players on all fours on the carpet, in the narrow space between the seats, and the teapot placed in the middle. Only four could play at a time, so Dan sat at the table to score. Barney also watched closely, and helped whenever he could by dashing after stray winks that pinged or rolled under the table, and scraping them back with his paw.

"Barney wishes he could play!" said
Freddie.

Jim showed outstanding talent. He
wasn't as quick moving around the floor as
the others, but his aim was
brilliant, even better
than Jenna's.
A cheer went
up each time he
flipped a wink into
the teapot where it
landed with a ringing
clatter. His best moment was when one
of his winks went in through the spout,
which Jenna said got him an extra two
points.

It was a tough final, between Jim and
Polly, but Polly's last two winks pinged into

the pot one after the other, and she was declared winner.

Dusk was falling by the time the game was over, and Jim said it was time to go back to *Whistling Jack*.

"It's our last day tomorrow," said Jenna, a little sadly. "The end of our holiday. We've got to take *Pernickety* back to the boatyard by lunchtime."

"We've got so used to living on a boat," Polly added, "it'll feel strange to go back to a house."

"In that case," said Jim, "you must all come and visit me and Barney on *Whistling Jack* some time soon. On one of the weekends when Freddie's with me. We'll play tiddlywinks again, if you bring the teapot. I'll look forward to the return fixture."

Everyone was happy with that. They all went out to the front deck; Barney jumped ashore, and Jim switched on his torch.

By its beam, Freddie saw something pink and shiny. His pig! He'd forgotten it again. He picked it up, tucking it under his arm. Then he followed Jim, ready to take a big step across to the bank.

Just as he pushed himself forward, there was a shout from Jenna. "The jigsaw! You've forgotten the jigsaw puzzle!"

"Oh! My present! How could I forget that?" Jim turned back, knocking into Freddie; Freddie overbalanced, and Jim grabbed his arm to steady him. The pig flew into the air, and landed in the water in front of the boat with a heavy *plosh*.

"Oh, no! Not again!" wailed Freddie.

"Pig overboard!" shouted Dan. He reached for the long pole kept on the roof, which had a hook on the end for fishing things out of the canal.

But Barney was faster. Without hesitation he launched himself in. The water was dark and cold and *wet*, streaming into his ears and his mouth. He didn't like it, but he wasn't going to let that pig go. No! Not after what had happened last time!

With no money inside it, the pig was lighter this time, bobbing on the surface. Barney paddled close, gripped its tail in his teeth, and swam for the bank. Everyone was watching him, cheering, and as soon as he swam close enough Jim reached down and lifted him out. He was shivering and dripping, but he still had hold of the pig, his teeth clamped tightly to its curly tail.

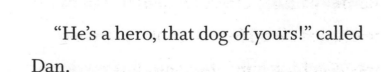

"He's a hero, that dog of yours!" called Dan.

"I know," said Jim.

Barney quite enjoyed all the fuss. He didn't particularly like having a shower, but at least the water in *Whistling Jack's* tiny bathroom was warmer and cleaner than the canal water. He did like being towelled dry by Freddie, while Jim prepared a dinner of meat and biscuits for him.

"Clever boy, Barney," Freddie told him. "You're the bravest and cleverest dog in the world."

There were times when Barney didn't *feel* very clever. Or very brave, either. He wasn't sure that he understood everything that had happened today.

But, when at last Jim and Freddie were in their beds, and the lights were turned off, and Barney snuggled by Freddie's feet on the top bunk, he did know that they were all together on *Whistling Jack*. The three of them.

And the pig.

Barney eyed it, where Freddie had stood it on the shelf after he'd dried it. It had a very smug, satisfied look on its face.

Barney was going to keep a close watch on that pig from now on, that was for sure. It was nothing but trouble, in his opinion.

Look out for
Barney the Boat Dog's
other adventures:

Usborne
Barney
The Boat Dog
Very Brave Dog
ISBN 9781409521983
Linda Newbery

Usborne
Barney
The Boat Dog
Runaway Horse!
ISBN 9781409521990
Linda Newbery

Usborne
Barney
The Boat Dog
Rescue Dog
ISBN 9781409522027
Linda Newbery

Cat Tales

Curl up with Cat Tales, also by
award-winning storyteller
Linda Newbery. Look out for:

The Cat with Two Names

Two of everything leads to double trouble for Cat...
ISBN 9780746096147

Rain Cat

Is the mysterious cat really controlling the weather?
ISBN 9780746097281

Smoke Cat

Where do the shadowy cats in next door's garden come from?
ISBN 9780746097298

Shop Cat

Strange things have been happening since Twister arrived...
ISBN 9780746097304

The Cat who Wasn't There

Who is the little white cat in Vincent's garden?
ISBN 9780746097328

Ice Cat

A cat made of snow and ice can't come to life...or can it?
ISBN 9780746097311

For more fun and furry
animal stories visit

www.fiction.usborne.com